Praise for Ia

"Maloney writes with panache ar
mundane circumstances."
Books on Asia

"As a writer he is bold, humorous and current."
The Japan Society

"Well, it's been a long, long time since I read a book where I felt as
charmed by a narrator as I did by Iain Maloney."
Will Heath, *Books and Bao*

Life is Elsewhere / Burn Your Flags

"A beautiful, brutal meditation on love and death and the death of
love. With these two compelling, tense, gorgeously-drawn and
perfectly-paced character accounts, giving each side of an unhappy
marriage, Iain Maloney has come into his own as a writer. From a
Japanese mountainside, to the forced bonhomie between ex-pats in
an Irish bar, to the angry intensity of feminist teenage punks in
Tokyo in the late 80s, this seemingly slight novella travels worlds and
light years in a few thousand words. Eri and Cormac, and all the
things they say and leave unsaid, will stay with you for a long time."
Kirstin Innes, author of *Scabby Queen*

"Maloney hits his stride here as he explores the tensions in a bi-
cultural relationship straining under marital irritations and life's
disappointments, all while the tedium of the pandemic presses down
on them like a long-suffering migraine. Follow Maloney's
experienced and knowing eye as he takes his readers back into a
world that other writers about Japan don't normally frequent – that
of punk-rock Tokyo in the late 1980s – where drugged-up young
women with electric blue hair and yellow Gibson guitars rant and
rage against the system. A raw yet compassionate take on a couple
trying to deal with their fears and frustrations, both with themselves
and with each other, in the time of Covid."
J. David Simons, author of *An Exquisite Sense of the Beautiful*

The Only Gaijin in the Village

"Intelligent, warm-hearted, down-to-earth and often very funny, *The Only Gaijin in the Village* is a very fine book."

Alan Spence, Edinburgh Makar, and author of *The Pure Land, Nightboat* and *Glasgow Zen*

"*The Only Gaijin in the Village* is a delightful tumble into village life, complete with a vivid cast of characters and a beautiful sense of place."

The Scotsman

"Juxtaposition of humor and insight proves to be the central pattern of the book. Each chapter is layered with shrewd observations about race, gender and generation, and cultural asides, all glued together with levity and distinctive social commentary... The finished memoir is a story that is indeed worth telling, a thought-provoking, lively examination of one immigrant's quest to create a new home outside his country of birth."

Kris Kosaka, *The Japan Times*

Fractures

"An emotional and physical journey that spans an entire year and at least two countries... this collection is rich with the unsaid."

The Japan Times

"The poems are full of wit and sincerity, with more variety than you'd expect from such short verse. A quick read initially, but one which pays again on revisits – highly recommended."

Russell Jones, author of *The Green Dress Whose Girl is Sleeping*

The Waves Burn Bright

"... a powerful portrayal of how the consequences of such a disruptive event can reverberate through people's lives for decades afterwards ... [the] characters are consistent, making believable, relatable choices."

The Herald

"Iain Maloney has done it again. He has written a book that simply must be read."
David Kenvyn, *For The Joy of Reading*

Silma Hill

"*Silma Hill* should be required reading."
Scotland on Sunday

"Recalling the likes of James Hogg's *Confessions*, George Douglas Brown's *The House with the Green Shutters*, and James Kelman's *How Late It Was How Late*... Maloney makes a memorable contemporary addition to rural Scottish Gothic."
Dr Neil Syme, University of Stirling

First Time Solo

"*First Time Solo* is an engrossing, consistently readable debut from a skilful and sensitive writer."
London Jazz News

"I found the book hard to put down... he left me wanting more."
Historical Novel Society

Also by Iain Maloney

Fiction

First Time Solo
Silma Hill
The Waves Burn Bright

Poetry

Fractures

Memoir

The Only Gaijin in the Village

Iain Maloney is from Aberdeen, Scotland, and lives in Japan.
iainmaloney.com
Twitter: @iainmaloney
Instagram: the_only_gaijin_in_the_village

First published 2021

Liminal Ink, Monifieth, UK
liminalink.com

Copyright © Iain Maloney 2021

A CIP catalogue reference of this book is available from the British
Library.

ISBN: 978-1-8381333-2-0
e-ISBN: 978-1-8381333-3-7

Printed and bound in Great Britain by Bell & Bain Ltd, Glasgow

Life Is Elsewhere/
Burn Your Flags

a novella

Iain Maloney

Liminal Ink

for Harrison

Life Is Elsewhere

Snow fell during the night, a sugar coating on the mountains. Frosted pine trees, an icy sheen on the clean, bright wood, yet even after the snow it's all still dusty scrub. These hills – hills, not mountains, whatever the tourist info says – are never going to inspire any great poetry. No hermits ever retreated to these sandy bumps to live out their lives in quiet contemplation. Lives of quiet desperation. Not here.

These aren't Mishima mountains where you can imagine the ill-fated world-rejected hero of a Mishima Yukio story coming to end it all, muscled torso exposed to the morning sun, a sharp blade – a meaningful blade, historical steel – cleansed and waiting, a suitable death poem on his lips. A romantic death. Meaningful death. Beautiful death.

You don't get beautiful deaths anymore. Not in 2020. You get deaths behind closed doors. Death behind plastic sheeting and infection controls. Death by statistics. Death by policy. The plague times. The end of days. No beautiful deaths, alone in an isolation room, a voice through an intercom. We built hospitals so we could keep death from our doors. Clean, tidy, elsewhere.

Life is elsewhere. I am elsewhere. But this year death is everywhere. Death is here.

On the way here I killed a snake. I saw it too late; a hosepipe stretched across the single-track road, just round the hairpin bend. My wheels were over it before I had time to register what I was seeing. Not even a dunt like in the movies, the sound of machine rolling over life, the jolt inside the car. Expensive suspension, thick tyres, a smooth ride. A shimahebi, harmless, but powerful, long. The head was moving, its back broken, flattened into the tarmac. I didn't know what to do so I left it. Another ugly death, alone and broken. Why did the snake cross the road? To get to the other side. Shouldn't go outside. Death is coming round every corner, silent.

I check my phone. Nothing. They said I'd get the results today. She'll call herself, Dr Endo, to deliver the news, good news, bad news. Either way, there will be news today. April 18, 1930 there was no news on the BBC. Here's some music instead. Music while you wait. Wait for the news. I looked on Wikipedia once about April 18, 1930. A typhoon made landfall in the Philippines, but that wasn't news-worthy in Britain then. Or maybe they didn't know. The news wasn't news then, it was always already yesterday's news. Yesterday, in the Philippines, a typhoon made landfall. We'll tell you how many died tomorrow. Now here's some music.

There's a website that tracks the cases, the deaths. One page, two counters, scrolling round, scrolling up, and up, and up. News in an instant. Up and up.

I don't usually climb in silence but I can't think of any sounds I want to hear. Nothing fits the mood but silence, the crump of my boots on the rocky path, the screech of those

Chinese birds wintering here. Noisy, brightly coloured. Stereotypes abound in nature. There was one other car in the car park, a white Kei truck, a tiny pickup, almost like a toy. Some old guy fishing, his camping stove and a frying pan, a one-cup sake and the din of family safely out of earshot. No one else on the paths. I have to keep reminding myself it's Christmas Day.

Back in Dublin, it's still Christmas Eve. Saoirse will be wrestling the kids into bed, stockings over the – where do you hang stockings if you don't have a fire? Off the bookcase? Stockings up, tree lights on, Santa on his way. A glass of wine, her and Gerry wrapping presents stashed on top of the wardrobe for a week at the most. Saoirse was always last-minute. Homework at school; ready for a date; driving me to the airport in March, the rush to get back to Japan before the borders closed. We only noticed as we came off the last roundabout that she still had her slippers on. You're getting just like Ma, I said. Well don't be telling Gerry that or he'll be off after a younger model. Just the excuse he needs, she said. Problems there? I asked. Nothing castration wouldn't solve, she said. And that's where you leave it because there were bigger problems than whether Gerry had been at it.

Only just got home. Japan closed the borders in March and us lifers weren't allowed back in until October and even then there were more hoops than at Celtic Park. Permanent residence. Contingent status. We're here under sufferance. Thanks for the taxes but once we perfect the robots, you'll not be needed. Right now entry to Japan is banned except for Japanese nationals. As if the virus checks your passport.

Eri picked me up, threw a mask at me, a bottle of hand gel, even though I already had both. Don't tell anyone where you've been, she said. Don't tell the neighbours you were in

Europe. Should I wear a badge? I said. Tattoo something on my forehead?

She wasn't laughing. She hasn't laughed much recently. Not much to laugh about. Even schadenfreude took a hammering this year. Can't laugh at the suffering of others when there's so much of it about. Where to start? Schadenfreude, like charity, starts at home. Laugh at thyself, you fucker, if you want something to laugh at. Christmas Day and you're on your own up in the hills. Not a present exchanged. Not even a merry or a happy. She was up late, locked in the spare room with her old boxes and that sake we got from Kochi, all of it. I could hear her snoring in there as I went downstairs and pulled my boots on.

Christmas really is fucking ridiculous when you think about it. Kids aside, of course. The niblings will be excited as anything for Santa and the works. Eighteen years in Japan and the word has lost all meaning. Grown-up adults decorating the house and putting on paper hats like they don't all hate each other 364 days. I kick a rock and before I realise it's gone over the edge and is tumbling down, gathering speed, gathering no moss. There's a golf course down there somewhere. Good. A rock, like the Indiana Jones rock at the start of *Raiders*, battering through the twelfth green, knocking some old executive in a pink cap and one glove flying.

A few Facebook Merry Christmases, a retweet of a retweet of a retweet. No news.

I stop and take a drink of water. It's even colder than when it came out the tap. Or maybe I'm just hotter. It's been a while since I got much above sea level. At the start of lockdown I did a bit, made myself get outside, but all the enthusiasm drained somewhere around June. Best intentions.

Every year Eri and I get in a couple of good hikes and

4

every year one of us says, we should keep it up this year, get fitter. We should have a goal. Maybe Kiso-Komagatake in the summer. Camp on the plateau like we did back in the day. Under the stars. By February I couldn't tell you whether the piping on my boots was red or yellow.

Shouldn't have taken the car. It's a faff with the trains but I hate retracing, going back. Makes the walk seem twice as long, half as interesting. Plus I could have a drink. A wee flask. A couple of cans. I know I shouldn't but it's Christmas. The Lord forgives a drink at Christmas. The Lord forgives but the body doesn't. The doctors won't.

Very, very cold water, water just above freezing, tastes of nothing, tastes of absence, tastes of the void. Swallow it inside me, swallow it down, taste the emptiness.

Hiking here is a recent import, 150 years or so. People climbed mountains, obviously, but mainly for religious reasons. Temples at the top, pilgrimages up the long and winding roads, barefoot, carrying a rock, devotional. Mental. No one did it for fun, as a hobby, as a way to fill the time while you're waiting. Not until some mad westerners showed up with poles and tennis rackets and buggered off up these divine slopes for a laugh. They didn't half embrace it, though, that mix of suffering and satisfaction potent, contagious and oh so human. Old women carrying enough equipment to restock basecamp for a forty-five minute round trip because you've gotta have the gear, and what's a climb without a cup of ramen at the top? Without a wee flask?

> on snow
> so easy
> to slip

I've always liked the haiku. It's what brought me to Japan in the first place. Like most men I had a Beat phase. *On The Road*, wine and jazz, girls and drugs, cut up and the best minds. But I never had much concentration for reading. Kerouac's haiku, that got me. That short sharp shock, the single moment, a story in a few words. Why does Tolstoy need so many when Bashō needs so few? Brevity is the soul of wit, said Shakespeare, so a haiku poet is wittier than a novelist. Joyce should've done *Ulysses* as a haiku.

> On June 16th
> Bloom had a shite
> Stephen had a drink
> Molly had a ride
> Yes, they did, yes.

Not really a haiku but there you go.

I write haiku in the hills. Write; not right. Don't write them down. I say them to the wind. Declaim them to the sky and then they are gone. About the moment; of the moment. There for a second, then gone. Haiku like cherry blossom. Writing them down is cheating, preserving something that claims to express the transient nature of existence.

> on snow
> so easy
> to slip

A wee flask. The little Jizō statue catches my eye, the tiny stone figure, a buddha, or a monk of some kind. A wee flask. A wee slip. So easy. But no, the flask is in the bar, on the shelf by the bottle of Bushmills. Three weeks without a drop. Must be the longest since I came of legal age. Three weeks. Two weeks, six days and some hours. Since the pain in the morning was too much to hide, to hide from her, from myself. Since I took myself to the clinic and Dr Endo took some blood, asked some questions, and scheduled me in for a scan. Yes, little Jizō-sama, no news, but the pain is still there, sometimes at the front, sometimes the side, mobile, a moveable feast, but always worse in the morning.

I didn't get anything for Eri. She didn't get me anything. I can't remember when we stopped buying each other presents. We used to, for sure, at the start. Then it became trips. I'd pay for a holiday around her birthday; she'd pay for one around mine. Bali. Seoul. Okinawa. An onsen in the hills. A cabin by the beach. Then we got busier and the trips became less frequent. I quit the teaching, opened the bar. We bought out the language school. Two businesses. No time for trips, for anything, for each other.

I got presents for the niblings. Books, Japanese snacks, things unremarkable to kids here, foreign and weird to my three wee Dubliners. Like me, their uncle Cormac who they are shy around every time we meet because a couple of years is forever at that age. Weird like me, a name at the edge of the map, where dragons be, their mother's brother on the far side of the world. A name. A concept. The reason Sean and Niall have to share a room for a few days when I'm home. A bringer of gifts; an inconvenience. He'll be gone soon, I heard her tell them at bedtime, the two of them taking their frustration out on each other. He'll be gone soon.

Well, maybe I will be, sister dear. Maybe I will. Wait and see what the good doctor has to say.

> this pack on my back
> this zen in my heart
> this rock in my head

Life Is Elsewhere

There's an old Zen story, a koan, a teaching. The nature of reality and the reality of nature. Where is that rock? says the master. Given the illusory nature of reality, says the student, that rock must be in my head. Very tiring, it must be, says the master who for me speaks like Yoda, to carry around a rock like that in your head. Reality is an illusion but we carry it with us. Learn to leave reality behind. Leave the rock behind. Life is tiring enough without dragging rocks.

If I were the student, I'd have smacked the master. Smug prick. Word play like that just makes the student feel stupid, pathetic, further than ever from their goal. What would the master have said if they'd given the other answer? Where is that rock? Over there by the cow. What smart-arse reply would have followed concerning the nature of the cow and the illusion of the rock? When there's no right answer, best to keep silent. Ignore the old fella. If the rock is an illusion then so are you, and your questions. What do you think, Jizō-sama? That's right – keep silent and smile. What else can you do?

>   this pack on my back
>   this zen in my heart
>   this rock in my head

This route is the long way round. You go over three peaks before coming down to the temple from the back. The first peak isn't even noticeable as a peak when you're on it. The hill is within the treeline and you'd miss the little shrine tucked away in the undergrowth if you didn't know it was there. The path meanders up and down so it's only when you reach the second peak and look back that you realise what you've already climbed.

The rocks are loose and flaky, the ground slips from under you. There are patches of snow off-piste, tufts of white like those appearing in my beard. In the distance the Southern Alps are snowbound, classical mountains with jagged summits and idiots sliding down them. Another import from the west. The trees either side are always trying to close the path, to bridge the gap. Roots poke out, crawl round outcrops. Leaves, berries, nuts litter the ground. In the brush there will be snakes, rodents, maybe even boar and bears. I should have a bell on my bag, to warn the bears. They should be hibernating but if they haven't eaten enough, haven't built up enough fat, they get desperate. Nothing more dangerous than a desperate bear. But I need peace and those bells get right on my nerves. Arhythmic jangling breaking the silence.

I never used to be this anti-social. You can't be if you run a bar. The chatter of your fellow man is money in the bank for a publican. But this year has done something to me, broken me. I look at people now and assess them for risk factors. Mask? Distance? Intentions? Any obvious signs of illness? I flinch when I hear a voice close to me. Something I'll need to get over if I'm ever to reopen the bar. Just now we have to close by 8.30pm, have customers separated by plastic screens. There's no point. It's cheaper just to close up, save on running costs. Who's done drinking by half eight? You're just getting going and it's last orders and masks on.

Eri's school is managing to hang on. One-to-one socially distanced lessons, discounted enough to overcome fear, the rest on Zoom. She had to let some of the teachers go but what can you do? It's hard for everyone. Gerry is working from home now as well. The world through Zoom, a little window to peer out of. At least he won't be doing his secretary, unless that's done through Zoom as well. Working from home makes wankers of us all.

Eri was saying, a couple of weeks back, that the masks are having an impact on the development of babies. It was in the news, apparently, or online somewhere, wherever she gets these things from. Eight-, nine-month-old babies have only ever seen a world masked up. Outside the house, no one has a face. Shock when someone outside takes their mask off to reveal something unexpected: a real human beneath the mask. I don't know how they know this, whether it was a study or just something someone reckoned, Eri didn't share her sources, but it got me thinking. Countries where they cover up, do they have this problem? Is there a developmental issue for children in places where women are covered head to toe? Teenage boys who have never seen the face of a woman they aren't related to. That must have an impact on outlook, expectations. Or is my ignorance leading to false conclusions? A blanket idea of what covered up means. Assumptions.

Before all this, masks were already common here. Have a cold; wear a mask to avoid spreading it. It also stops people seeing your red nose, the chapped lips, dried snot and raw nostrils. I wear a mask to stop catching things, even if they are only partially effective. All those anti-maskers: if it isn't 100% effective, it isn't worth it. So stop using chemical cleaners (kills 99% of all known germs), stop using insurance (doesn't cover 100% of claims), and stop using condoms (97% protection). I'm sure if you offered Gerry a 3% chance of getting his secretary pregnant against a 50% chance, he'd bite your hand off. Although that must be a giveaway. I haven't owned a condom in ten years, not since we knew we couldn't have kids. If I suddenly had one in my wallet, what a giveaway! How can people be bothered to have affairs? Is the reward really worth the effort?

We wear masks in hay fever season to keep the pollen out. Teenagers wear masks to hide their spots. Wish I'd known that when I was a pizza-faced teen. Women wear masks on no-make-up days. The shy wear masks. Now everyone wears a mask and babies think it's normal. The world to them is faceless, blank, empty.

Two years ago we had a party for my fortieth. Back when parties were a thing. Friends over, barbecue in the garden, drinking until late. Coping fine with turning forty, or at least I thought I was. I came in for more ice and found Eri looking at herself in the hall mirror. She pulled out the bobble holding her hair back, slipped it onto her wrist, pushed her hair into different styles, put it up again, scraped it back, let it drop with a sigh.

'When did I get so fucking old?'

'Slowly. Over time.'

'Very funny. I need to dye my hair again.'

'It is dyed.'

'Yes, it's dyed. It's dyed the same acceptable, respectable colour that everyone else's hair is dyed.'

She looked at me in the reflection for a moment, and then back at herself.

'Did you see Honoka's dyed hers the same colour as mine? Why can't she ever do anything original? Why can't anyone? You should go to a salon in spring and see all the newly-graduated high school girls come in. They aren't allowed to dye their hair while they're at school so the first thing they do when they are released into the world is rebel. They go to the salon in a bid to differentiate themselves, and each one comes out with the same rust brown. This fucking colour.' She flicks one side of her hair up in disgust. 'We're all rebelling by doing exactly the same thing.'

'Did you do that? Go to the salon after high school?'

'You know I didn't graduate high school.'

'Yes. Sorry. When did you first dye your hair?'

'When I was fifteen. Maybe fourteen?'

'Rust brown?'

'Green and gold.' She smiled at the memory. 'When did I become respectable? When did that happen?'

'You couldn't be a punk forever.'

'Why not? That's the point of punk. It's a way of life, a philosophy.'

'The Tao of Rotten.'

'I'd be more of a rebel if I just let my natural colour grow in. Maybe I'll cut it short again. Or get an undercut.'

'You could shave it completely. A rebel with a crew.'

'If I shaved my head you'd be out the door before the last hair touched the bathroom floor.' She straightened her shoulders, pushed her breasts up, held the position for a moment then sank against my shoulder. 'I think I'm having a midlife crisis.'

'You're only thirty-nine. Japanese women live forever.'

'They stay alive forever, but most of them have dementia.'

'Yōko Ono is eighty-five and is still punk. You're still punk. Punk as fuck.'

'I run a language school. I wear a suit to work. I have a mortgage. None of those are punk as fuck.'

'So what do you want to do? Quit?'

'Maybe.'

'We can afford it. Take a step back. Kyoko can run things.'

'I'll think about it. Did you see on the news that an elderly woman with dementia walked in front of a train?'

'You're a long way from walking in front of trains.'

I first met Eri in a music venue, a live house called Club Rock N Roll. A friend of mine played drums in Oblivion, a short-lived grunge band. Grunge was long dead, but this four-piece didn't give a fuck, which suited me fine. The world would be a much better place today if the nineties had never ended.

There were three other bands on the bill, two local, one through from Osaka. I don't remember much about them because I spent most of the evening sitting at the bar chatting up the barmaid: Eri.

She was something back then. Her hair was silver, this extra-terrestrial, seventies science fiction silver, centre-parted in a bob that stopped at the bottom of her ears, sharp-edged like it had been razored. It was undercut on either side, the shaved parts flashing when she swung her head to locate a bottle opener or a knife for the lemons. I drank Heineken after Heineken trying to keep her attention in what I thought, can after can, was increasingly fluent Japanese.

My friend's band was on last and when I heard their opening tape – a recording of feedback overlaid with Eddie Vedder's 1996 Grammy acceptance speech – *I don't know what this means... I don't think it means anything. That's just the way I feel* – I jumped up from the bar, knocking over the pyramid of cans I'd built next to me and dived into the eight-person mosh pit.

Afterwards, sweaty, ears ringing, high on the band, the set, just the experience of live music, I asked for her phone number and got shot down. The band invited me out with them and a crowd of others to keep drinking. We went to an izakaya and stocked up on fried chicken to soak up the booze, then on to karaoke. I was doing the Pixies' 'Where is My Mind' when someone started joining in on the 'ooh-oohs'. Eri. She'd finished work and caught up with the band. She was friends with Oblivion's lead guitarist, Asuka, who also worked in Club Rock N Roll. Many drinks. Many songs. Somehow we ended up in Tsurumai Park as the sun came up. Four of us, then three, finally just me and her, cans of coffee as the world went to work around us.

Life Is Elsewhere

this forest
a life here
a moment

The wind takes my words away, over the trees and out to sea.

Forty was like a flicked switch, where everything started going wrong. Probably confirmation bias but it does feel like the day after my birthday all these aches and pains appeared. First it was a pain in the chest on the left side, just above my heart. Probably muscular. I'd get indigestion every other day. A pain in my toe that might have been gout. It went and never came back. Numbness in my right leg. I was woken one night with a sharp pain right where my liver is. This year I haven't been able to shit. One day constipated, the next flowing like a deforested mountain after a typhoon.

Something seemed to change in our relationship after that conversation in the mirror. We argue more than we used to. Seem to take delight in prodding the other until they react. Pushing buttons just because the buttons are there. We both took refuge in work. I stayed over at the bar rather than coming home. We texted each other rather than speaking. Then lockdown hit, the bar closed and I was at home every day.

I try. I make an effort. But she focuses on all my failings. She doesn't say anything but I can see what she's thinking. Another drink. Another helping. More weight. More weight. Health deteriorating but it's all my fault. Rather than air her disgust with me she says nothing. Silence. The house has become silent. She turned the spare room into an office so she could work from home and stays in there from morning to night. Now she's sleeping in there.

this forest
a life here
a moment

I could stay here. A tent. Build a shelter. Live out my days in the woods, peaceful, silent, alone. She could get on with her life. Return to her roots, the free spirit, the punk, without carrying my dead weight around, this rock in her head.

The last time I saw Mike we spoke about going to Mars. There'd been something on the news about manned missions, and how they were looking for couples in their fifties who had been together for decades. The length of the trip, the proximity, the stress, the crew had to be able to put up with each other and who better than married couples who have put up with each other's crap for decades. That and the one-way nature of the whole enterprise. In a moment of clarity, Mike asked if Eri and I would do it. I'd be up for it, I said. But she wouldn't go. Even as I said it, I knew that was a lie. It would be the other way around. She's the adventurous one, the one able to leave everything behind and start again. She's done it before. More than once. I started a new life here but have always kept one eye on Ireland. Saoirse is like an anchor there. I didn't cut all ties like Eri did. I just let out more rope. Who was I kidding, thinking I could ever go to Mars? I asked Mike if he'd go, but he'd taken another hit on his pipe and there was no getting sense out of him. That night I asked the regulars, the bar staff. We discussed the pros and cons, but Shiori summed it up in her flat refusal: I wondered why, was it the knowledge that you'd never come back, that you'd die millions of miles from home, that maybe you'd never even make it? 'No,' she said. 'Earth is just much more convenient.'

Life Is Elsewhere

a new path on a familiar mountain
like meeting for the first time   again

The summit of the second peak is more what you'd hope it would be: above the treeline, a cairn of stacked rocks, a wooden shelter and a view over trees, the slash of the river through the pine canopy, the white peaks on the horizon. The wind is brutal up here, exposed and open. Winter here is mostly dry, but by Christ it's cold. This wind rips across Russia and China from the Arctic and gets right into my bones. Growing up in Ireland should have prepared me for this but again age is changing the rules. This winter I've found myself scared to go outside, actually living in fear of the cold. There's no such thing as bad weather, just bad clothes. Now I pour more kerosene into the heater and order more long-johns from Uniqlo. A wee flask would go down well now.

I take a photo and send it to Saoirse. Christmas in Japan. They'll all be asleep now, warm in the central heating, the turkey prepped in the fridge, the beer stacked in the garage. That warmth sounds inviting. Maybe Eri will be up for some dinner later. I could make a stew, or roast something. Winter food, hot and filling. We could watch something together on Netflix, side by side on the sofa, rather than watching our own programmes on separate iPads. We could, if it's good news.

No missed calls. No messages. Full reception. Battery at sixty-seven percent. Just a normal Friday for Dr Endo.

It's been eighteen months since that conversation with Mike about going to Mars. I said it was the last time I saw him but that's a lie. It's the last time I saw him before the airport. So that would be fifteen months since I last saw him; since he disappeared.

16

I'd been getting increasingly worried about him. He was a skater, a surfer, a stoner, always capable of drifting off, changing lanes, acting outright bizarre, but that new shit was messing him up. He and Kana had got married and she was trying to get him to stop smoking pot. She was fine with the drug itself – she'd lived in Australia with him, smoked a few bowls herself – but getting caught in Japan wasn't worth the risk, and being married to a convicted drug user is not something a reputation can survive in Japan. If he got caught, it would be over for both of them. So he fixated on the legality of the thing and decided to get clean by swapping his illegal high for the newly-available legal highs in the head shops around Osu. We only found out later that the base for these legal highs was ketamine. Trying to get off pot by getting into ketamine is just insane, regardless of technical legality.

He used to be such a good laugh, if always a bit unreliable. One of the first people I met in Japan, one of my oldest friends here. We were in the same JET intake, training together, teaching in nearby schools. He'd been to Japan before, had studied Japanese at university, knew folk, skaters mainly, local lads to go drinking with. Through them I met the musicians, the bands, got into the scene. None of this without him.

We used to have these wild nights. The summer was always the best, with the festivals, the fireworks.

The first summer. We find a space on the stone steps down from the castle and sink, exhausted, crack our beers and light our fags. Above us the pink and white cherry blossom puff like popcorn in the wind, the moonlight melancholy on the petals. The smell of frying chicken, of baking pancakes, of sweets I couldn't name with flavours I couldn't place has dissipated. Children ran between the shrines at the foot of Inuyama

Castle, the stone bridge that leads nowhere, the lines of red torii gates and dog statues, lanterns and stalls, but now they're in bed, the town silent but for the sound of a lighter sparking, a can cracking, the scrape of Converse on granite steps. Plywood prayers clap, layers of wishes. We were sitting there half a day earlier watching the marionette performance on top of one of the traditional festival floats that were pushed and pulled from their towering garages through the narrow streets of the old town and parked before the castle while their teams indulged in udon and sake. Spring is officially here, and that is reason enough to celebrate.

I untie a red and blue Chunichi flag from a fence, still unsure if it is the flag of the local area, the local paper or the baseball team; tie it to the end of a bamboo pole Jeff took from one of the ukai fishing boats down by the bridge. 'Come on.'

Through the shrines and torii the path curves to the right, climbing. I lead the way, bamboo flagpole raised aloft, the tip catching on branches, swaying as I lurch from side to side. Watching the flag flutter directly above makes me dizzy. 'Fuck, I'm gonna throw.'

Mike continues on ahead, passing the ticket booth. I wipe my mouth on some leaves, spit acid into the bushes. I never eat enough at these things, picking at fried chicken and half-cooked sausages, pouring cans of overpriced Asahi into my face. Every festival, I never learn. I catch up with Jeff and pull a can from his backpack.

'Where did Mike go?'

'Fuck knows. Having a slash?'

'Fuckers! Up here!'

About fifteen feet above us, Mike stands on the top of the castle's outer wall, balanced on the ornate tiles, his cock out, an arc of piss walking its way towards us.

We jump back, avoid the splashes. Jeff picks up a decent-sized pebble, takes aim and lobs it at Mike. He misses, the stone disappearing over Mike's shoulder with a clatter.

'How did you get up there?'

'Follow the wall along there. There's a drainpipe.'

'Here, grab this,' I say, waving the flagpole at him.

'That's what your mother said.'

'Fucking take it.'

'She said that, too.'

Jeff appears on the wall, a leg either side. Mike surfs and skates, seems quite happy with the height, still has confidence in his co-ordination. Jeff is under no such illusions. With his beard, checked shirt and outsize frame, he's more lumberjack out on a limb than ninja penetrating a castle. Mike finally takes the flag from me and waves it about, reaching above the trees. He brings it down, rapidly swinging it through the air towards Jeff, whipping the flag over his head like a matador.

'I'm going to take great delight in watching you fall off here.' Jeff ducks again but grabs the pole as it passes him, yanks it then pushes it back, hard. Mike gets it in the stomach and drops off the wall, into the castle.

'Fuck! Jeff, is he alright?' Shimmy along the wall to the drainpipe and haul myself up. I haven't done this since I was a kid but the principle is the same, toes on the brackets and pull. Don't stop till you're at the top. I flop over and put a leg either side, same as Jeff, get my breath back. My throat raw from vomit. Once balanced I look up. Jeff's looking back over his shoulder at me, grinning. Mike stands on the gift shop roof, about three feet lower than the main wall, the middle finger of each hand raised in greeting.

'Prick.'

Jeff slides along and follows him down, me behind them both. Inside, the castle keep seems eerie, just us alone in the dark. The tower stronger and more impressive in silhouette than during the day. One of four originals in Japan but only the tower remains, so it's usually hard to get a sense of the power that once resided here. Not now. From this side the hill rises slowly but beyond the castle is a steep cliff down to the river, a drop no one could survive. From the other side of the river, the castle stands aloft, overseeing everything. There's real history in the ground, murmuring under the crunch of gravel.

The castle itself is locked and Mike's shoulder doesn't even make it shiver. I take up the fallen flag and head over to the far corner, beyond the lightning tree. There's a viewpoint, a fenced-off area where you can sit and watch the river unfurling, Narita-san Temple on the opposing mountain. I climb up onto the picnic bench and slip the pole through the parasol hole in the wood. Leans too much. I jump down and scrabble for a stone the right size to wedge it in place.

'Hang on.' Jeff gets his camera out, the massive SLR he carries everywhere, fiddles with the settings and lenses. 'Mike, get up there with him. No, on the bench. Cormac, you get up on the table.'

I see what he's getting at and remove the pole, pushing the end down past Mike. 'Hold that there, and I'll go under here, like it's heavy and we're raising it. Shame there aren't more people.'

'For what?' Mike pins his cigarette between his lips and takes the pole with two hands.

'Iwo Jima,' says Jeff, and starts snapping.

We defined ourselves by the good times; thought they'd never end. Keith Richards never talks about the aches, the scares, the scans and the talks. It's just fun, fun, fun. Smoking ketamine is a pretty fucking dumb thing to do but we delude ourselves with addicts' logic.

Mike disappeared from the bar one night. Said he was going to the toilet. It was only about forty minutes later that Leah, her turn at the open mic done, asked where he was. Called him but his phone rang from his jacket on the bar stool. We shrugged and got on with the evening. Another hour or so later he wandered back in as if nothing had happened.

'Where the fuck have you been?'

He glances over at Leah, who rolls her eyes and goes over to the sound booth. She knows I'll tell her everything later anyway.

'Give me a Cuba libre. Easy on the libre.'

I mix it up, make one for myself.

'So?'

'I went home.'

'Melbourne?'

'No, the apartment. Obviously.'

No sense of humour tonight. I sip.

'I think Kana is sleeping with someone else.'

'Fuck. Really?'

'Yeah. I thought she'd be with him tonight so I went home to catch them.'

'You thought they were fucking at yours? Shit, man. Were they?'

'I think so. I got there and listened. Waited until a train went past and used the noise to cover turning the key and opening the door.'

'Classic. And?'

'She was watching TV.'

'By herself?'

'So it seemed.'

'You think he was hiding?'

'Must have been. I looked but I couldn't find him.'

'Maybe he was never there?'

'He must have been.'

'Why?'

'I heard someone talking about it.'

'Shit. Who? Where?'

'The people in the apartment above. They were talking about it. Laughing at me. One was saying that she's fucking some guy at work, how it made much more sense than being with a fucking druggie loser like me.'

'You could hear them?'

'Yeah. I recorded them on my phone.' He takes it out but doesn't play it. 'And the other day, when we were having sex. She started playing with herself, you know? She'd never done it before. And I never told her to do it. She must have learned it from someone else.'

'She could've just wanted to come and your tiny dick wasn't going to do the business.' Humour isn't cutting through. I drain my glass, tap it against his. 'Another?' He seems to notice it for the first time, takes a big gulp.

'All right if I smoke in here?'

I shrug. 'I'd rather you just drank.'

'I need to calm down, man.'

'That's what I mean.'

It's a pretty steep route down the cleavage of the second mountain and up to the final peak. I run that conversation over in my head, amazed at how relaxed I was at the time. He'd admitted to hearing voices but I hadn't heard him say it. I was so used to not really taking in the mad shit he said I didn't notice when he started saying actually mad shit.

It was Kana who finally pointed out the obvious to us all.

She took me round to the flat. Said it was important but wouldn't tell me why. He'd trashed the place. Properly trashed it. Fridge freezer was on its front, wires pulled out of the back. Every window smashed, the mirrors and TV, too. Carpet up. Holes in the walls and ceilings. Every room utterly destroyed. The owner would need to rebuild from scratch before renting it out again. He was searching, she said. Searching for recording devices. Searching for speakers. Trying to find out where the voices were coming from. Tracking them down to the source. The voices that told him Kana couldn't be trusted, that Kana was cheating on him, that the world was against him.

I took her back to the bar – closed at that time of day – and together we made a plan. We had to get him out of the country. Japan doesn't do rehab, it just does jail. He needed help, and he could get that in Australia. She called his folks. I called him.

After hours of trying I finally got him to answer his phone. He came into the bar, looking and smelling like shit. He'd got a scooter from somewhere, was riding around town off his tits for days. We got lucky; he was lucid and agreed to be helped. I booked him a flight. Now all we had to do was get him to the airport.

Kana packed his things, found his passport. I kept him in the bar, kept the bar closed. I let him carry on smoking that shit because otherwise he'd have been off, gone for good. The flight was at seven the next morning, and Kana and I stayed awake the whole night. We got him to the airport. Got him to ditch his pipe after he'd sucked up the last of the drugs. We got him checked in. Then he tried to run. I caught up with him, pulled him out of a taxi and took him back, got him through security. The last thing I said was, 'I love you, man. I'll see you when you're better.' Then I ran. I ran and grabbed Kana and put her in the car and took off. Her phone was ringing, Mike calling saying he'd changed his mind. Texting abuse. I took her phone and threw it in the back. I wasn't stopping for anything. Security could deal with him.

He got on the plane. His family picked him up and took him to rehab. Three days later he ran off. For some reason no one had taken his passport. He got the first flight back to Japan and hasn't been seen since.

Scientists used to think drugs caused mental illnesses like schizophrenia. Now the thinking is people predisposed to certain conditions are attracted to certain drugs. I smoked a bit at uni but it never really did much for me, just made me sleepy. Alcohol, however, lights me up like a Christmas tree. Mike was different. He could take or leave drink, but marijuana interacted with his wiring in a way that was very much to his liking. The ketamine cracked open a door already ajar. I wonder where he is this Christmas.

> I envy the seasons
> their second chances

We're all wearing masks. Mishima knew all about that. His *Confessions of a Mask* mines the tensions of his youth for art – a very Japanese thing, where the line between the life of an author and his work is literally paper thin – and peels back some of the layers in his own life. A gay man in a traditional patriarchal society. A man who romanticised the military life – from samurai to modern soldiers – while avoiding military service through a mixture of genuine illness and a bit of fakery. His guilt at sitting out the war, while the rest of his generation died in jungles and mountains and oceans, led to him fantasising endlessly about the heroic, romantic, beautiful death. The sword in the stomach, the opening of yourself to the outside, one final mask removed in that moment before the second sword slashes down and takes your head, the second sword that acknowledges the reality of seppuku, that spilling your guts is slow and painful and as far from beauty as one could imagine. The heroic death. The romantic death. Face down in a pool. On your back choking on vomit. A needle in your arm, a gag in your mouth, your liver exploding as you watch TV. The romantic death, the beautiful death. Mishima's heroic death was met with laughter.

When mankind wails, nature laughs.

> this pack on my back
> this zen in my heart
> this rock in my head

On the third peak I stop for a rest. The highest point in this tiny range; the only summit more than 500 metres high. An older man disappears down one path as I emerge from mine, and I have the place to myself. He must have heard me coming, knew I'd ruin his solitude. I take out a rice ball and some chocolate, check my phone. Still nothing. I text Eri, *dinner tonight?*

There's an angle from where you can imagine what this area was like before industrialisation. If you stand just so, and keep your eyes fixed on one point of the horizon, nothing as far as your peripheral vision shows any signs of modernity. Trees, mountains, the river. Sky, clouds, birds. Stones, dirt, water. How the world would look without us. We are visitors on this spinning rock. We could fly off into the stars and nothing would mourn us. We have dominion over nothing. One tiny virus and the world slams to a halt. All the things we were told were inevitable, all the systems and structures and assumptions, the end of history and the peak of progress, all a house of cards built on clouds. If you stand just so, and look ahead, you can see it all gone. The world, rolling on without us. Extinctions come and go. Romantic deaths, beautiful deaths, heroic deaths. A line in the rocks; none shall pass. Life is elsewhere.

A message. Eri: *I'm not cooking.*

First response, defensive, negative. Like back home. Didn't notice it until I came here, how negative we are. The first response to anything is negative. Here's something I just learned that may be new to you. *That's a load of shite.* Let's go somewhere different. *Everywhere's shite.* Let's try that new place. *I've heard it's shite. There's no good music these days. Kids are getting worse. It'll all end in tears.* The biggest obstacle to happiness is our own comfort in misery.

I'm not cooking.

I'll cook. Was thinking about a stew. Warm winter food.

I might have to go out.

Let me know.

No reply. Silence.

The temple sits on a promontory about halfway up the mountain. You can't see it from the top because of the folds of the cliffs, and you can't see it from the bottom because of the treeline. It's perfectly hidden yet the views across the land are remarkable. People come from miles around to see the autumn leaves from here, but in winter it has the air of abandonment. The monks attached to it live and work in a compound further around the mountain, out of sight of the main shrine. Even though you are technically never alone, it can often feel like it.

In my mind, the temple precinct is divided into three areas. There's the visitors' bit, which encompasses the car park, toilets, shop selling charms and beads, the viewpoint where the crowds gather for the leaves. I avoid these parts as much as possible, which is why I come the long way round. The stairs are lined with stone idols in their distinctive red aprons, by small shrines to other gods, and punctuated by statues of the seven lucky gods, Ebisu, Daikokuten, Bishamonten, Benzaiten – the only goddess, devoted to wisdom, art and beauty, depicted as a sensual woman playing the shamisen – Hotei, Fukurokuju and Jurōjin. At New Year they come in their treasure ship, distributing presents. They'll come again, soon, and the children will get little envelopes of cash.

Then there are the temple buildings, which are ignored by most visitors. To be honest, the temple's not all that to look at. Plain wood, the usual curved eaves. Bit of a gold bodhisattva, huge bell. Shrines are torn down and rebuilt every twenty years as part of a tradition of purification, and this incarnation is still new enough to be clear of moss and water marks. The shrine itself is two buildings connected by a low walkway. When it's quiet, you often find cosplayers using the temple and especially the bell as a backdrop to their photos. I got quite the surprise the first time I came down off the mountain to discover a group of young men and women dressed as characters from anime and manga posing all over the temple. They seemed just as startled by my presence so we respectfully left each other alone.

The third area is my area. My Mishima area. The path up the mountain is invisible from the temple; you have to know it's there to find it. But coming down, this isn't a problem. The first you know about the impending temple is the increase in the number of little Jizō-sama statues lining the road. The cliffs get steeper and sharper, so there are ropes to hang onto and, in one place, a ladder bolted to the rock face. The first time I nearly turned back, wondering what I'd got myself into. You don't expect to need climbing gear in hills this low.

Once you're over the last drop and onto the flat ground, you're in amongst an unkempt and apparently forgotten cemetery. Memorial slabs covered in moss, stone lanterns, depictions of deities and demons. If you came upon this unexpectedly at night, you'd be well within your rights to freak out.

The path seems to disappear. You meander across the dirt, still unaware you are about to trip over a temple. The trees hang low: a green marquee, sky obscured, no horizon but leaves. If I ever end up homeless in Japan, this spot is where I'd go first. A Robin Hood hideaway. To the right a set of steps becomes visible. Ignore them. They lead to the tourists. Go the other way, and paradise is found.

A stream running down the mountain that you've stepped over countless times as it twists around the path into a natural pond before flowing out again over the edge, a narrow waterfall dropping four or five metres. The pond isn't visible from the temple – few know it's there and it's always quiet. On a tiny island, no more than a jutting rock, stands a red shrine. An arched bridge loops over the stream where it widens into the pond.

At the far end, about two metres along from the waterfall, the cliff edge folds and pokes out above the valley a couple of hundred metres below. This is my spot. This is where I sit, Jizō-sama to my back, pond to my left, and sink into the silence of reality.

> this pond   the next
> a torrent builds
> tumbling

Today, some snow still covers the rocks around my spot. I drop my pack and kneel down, scoop the snow together and build a snowman, no bigger than the Jizō-sama watching me. In Japanese, the word for snowman is yukidaruma. Snow Buddha.

The daruma comes from the Bodhidharma, the monk credited with founding Zen Buddhism. Dharma in the Japanese syllabary becomes da-ru-ma. Daruma. Round, red, bearded Daruma dolls are sold at many temples and are considered good luck charms. I think this name, yukidaruma, may be my favourite thing about Japan. Snowman is so prosaic, unimaginative. Snow Buddha. Snow Dharma. That's got poetry to it, a name in touch with wider ideas, more than just a descriptive label. I build my snow buddha and together we look out over the valley, the pine trees, the rush of the waterfall. Come on, Snow Buddha, bring me luck. Dr Endo must ring soon.

> I try to catch my breath;
> the river has already moved on

The founder of this temple was a monk said to have special powers when it came to fighting disease and sickness. He could turn himself into some kind of demon and defeat the yakubyo-gami: disease-causing being, or Pestilence in the Christian tradition. Stencils of his demonic form are sold in the gift shop. He is by no means the only monk to whom these powers are attributed across Japan, but he founded this place and this is my spot.

I need his help today. My yukidaruma and I, we need his help. Snow Buddha will melt before too long and me, well, my future hangs in the balance of a phone call. Dr Endo's Christmas gift to me.

> maple leaf in the ripples
> beneath a setting sun

I'll need beef for the stew. Or maybe lamb. The only place that sells lamb is Costco and I'm not going there on Christmas

Day. Beef from the butcher, the good stuff. Potatoes, carrots, garlic and rosemary, all from the garden. A bottle of Guinness for taste. One for the stew, one for me.

No.

Wait for Dr Endo. See what she says.

No.

Where is Mike today? Do his parents know? Kana has no idea. She says she got their marriage annulled. I don't know about the logistics of this but I imagine telling the city office 'I married a foreign drug addict by mistake, please help me' would push the paperwork through.

Could I have done more? Should I have done more? He was blasting ketamine in my car in the car park of an international airport. If we'd been found, if he'd been caught, I'd have been arrested right alongside him. No ifs, no buts. I'd have been arrested and either jailed here or deported. My life over, my marriage over, my business taken from me. It was fear, self-preservation. I ran, shoved Kana in the car and ran. When I got home, Eri was in a panic. I should never have taken him to the airport. I should never have got so involved. He did it to himself, she said. It's his own fault. And Kana's fault for marrying him. But not ours. The coincidence of our friendship did not mean I had any part to play in saving him from himself.

She loved me then, that day. She loved me when she thought she could lose me. But that love harboured anger. Mike put us in that situation and rather than think of our marriage, I thought of friendship. The bonds and responsibilities of male friendship. Perhaps I made a choice that day without ever realising. I thought I was walking the line, helping a mate by pushing him away. But did I push her away at the same time? Should I have been more ruthless? You did this to yourself, mate. What did you think would happen, smoking fucking ketamine?

There's a pain in my right side, just below the ribs. Insistent, burning.

He did it to himself, and now he's on his own.

> two rocks wade in the same water
> under autumn leaves

The waterfall keeps flowing. There's a hard edge, a rock wall that stops the whole pond flooding over in one explosive outburst. The water seeps at just the right pace to keep the pond full but not overflowing. Did the monk do that? Did nature? It's balanced that way but it wouldn't take much to upset the equilibrium. Displacement. Removal. Change one variable and the whole pond could drain away.

The maple leaves in the pond drift and float in the eddies. They clump together in channels, pile against rocks, sheltering. Some give in to the torrent and go over, tumbling through the air. This is my place, my Mishima Mountain dais. This is where I'd do it. The sun rising, white bandana around my head, shirt folded on a nearby rock. With the Jizō-sama and Snow Buddha watching, I'd take water from the pond and run it over the blade. Point against my abdomen, death poem on my lips. A shout, a sigh, a lunge, body onto steel, steel into my body. No second, no sword swinging down, just this winter sun low above the hills as my body slumps onto the rocks, then tips over the edge, tumbling with the maple.

> on snow
> so easy
> to slip

I'll call Saoirse later. Make an effort with Eri tonight. Keep my temper. I won't give in to despair. I'll react positively, even when faced with negativity. Make a special dinner and I won't touch a drop. Go to the gift shop and buy a stencilled demon and hang him above the door. We'll keep illness at bay for another year. We've survived this year. The vaccines are coming. In the spring I'll reopen the bar. We can take a trip, go to Hieizan, or Tokyo, or Ireland. Timbuktu. Tipperary. It's a long way. We can throw off our masks, show the newborns we all have faces. We'll be together again, be social. I'll stop being afraid of noise, of contact. I'll get used to being around others again. I'll go to the gym, eat better, kick the drinking once and for all. I'll donate money to this temple. Money to charities. I'll reach out to Kana, see if she's okay. I'll give money to places that help drug addicts. I'll lose my masks, all my masks, and be open and honest with Eri, with everyone, with the world. If only. If only there's good news.

A fish jumps in the pond, catches an insect and splashes back. The chirp of birds. Somewhere, the rumble of a train. There's a small puddle under the yukidaruma, a rivulet down his rock.

> this pack on my back
> this zen in my heart
> this rock in my head

My phone rings.

Burn Your Flags

Ipour myself a glass of our homemade plum wine, top it up with tonic water, a handful of ice. The house creaks along with the ice. It's about twenty years old. Younger than I am. Older than I am. Depending on which me we're talking about. Eri Kennedy. Eri Kanehara. The one before that. I creak, too, when I move. When I wake in the morning, still on my side of the bed even though he's not there, my legs are so stiff, like I ran a marathon the day before, climbed Ontake. Is it age? Bad health, something I've done to myself, living too fast for too many years? This house and I, both of us are creaking and groaning. One day we'll fall down, nothing but rubble and dust.

It's Christmas Eve and Cormac is out. The place feels empty when he's not here, which I hate to admit, but it does. He fills a room, fills a house. The smell of him. The sound of him doing the dishes, tutting and sighing at something I've left half-done. His music. His TV shows. Always his choices. When he's not here he's still here. A negative, an unavoidable hole. When he's not here because he's deliberately being not here. When he's making a point of being elsewhere. Rather than be here. Rather than dealing with this. I wish he'd come home angry. Come in and shout. Slam doors. Put his fist through the wall. Something. Instead he just disappears, sinks into the routine of his work, of running the bar, cleaning the pipes, ordering stock. All rather than confront what's going on. Confront the inevitable.

At the start of lockdown he was optimistic, kept the bar open. Then it sunk in, he closed up, used up the perishable stock, and suddenly he was home every day. Here, under my feet, in my face. We both had work to fill the silence, and now he has no work to do, I have no work to go to. I understand it now, all those women who divorce when he retires. A lifetime of him doing nothing but eating and sleeping, little more than an ill-tempered lodger who brings in the money and then suddenly he's there, all day, every day. This man you've grown old ignoring. This man who only now notices the kids have left. And you can't take it, can't take this man, used to being obeyed in the office, not having an outlet for his bullying. Thank god for golf.

I thought I'd avoided all that, marrying a foreigner. But it's not nationality, it's gender. It's the whole fucking lot of them.

He's out somewhere. Mooching in the empty bar. Maybe, just maybe, at the gym. My phone chimes. That'll be him. He can't go five minutes without saying something. He used to touch me all the time, every time he walked past me, like he was checking I was real, that I was still there. When did he stop? It isn't from him. There are some Facebook notifications, new Tweets as always, the red bubbles climbing and climbing, reminders there are still people out there, trying to be social, a reminder that I am avoiding them all. It isn't from him. It's an email. When I see the name I nearly drop the phone. Kat. Kat Higueros Hayashida.

Iain Maloney

My finger hovers over her name.

I thought I saw her. Manako, a flash of her neon blue hair in a shop window. A reflection; her ghost. Tiny izakaya bars and ramen restaurants. Faded neon and false noise. That smile, the laughter lines widen, a glimmer in those hazel eyes. Two women with new hair out on the town. In my head I'm still young, still a teenager. The woman in the window is old enough to have adult kids. A ripple in the background, something electric flashes by.

The ghosts are out tonight.

Dear Eri,

You are Eri now, aren't you? This is you, isn't it? Your photo is on the website of your language school. I know it's you.

How are you? I'm in Berlin now, doing session work, mostly. I hope you're surviving these awful times.

Sorry to get in touch out of the blue, but something's happened you should know about. As you know, next year will be the twenty-fifth anniversary (anniversary, is that the right word?). Someone's making a documentary about her and the band. I guess I figured this would happen but it was still a surprise when it did. Dylan Charles, have you heard of him? Anyway, he's sniffing around, trying to interview everyone involved. He contacted me, and he's looking for you. I've agreed to meet him — just to see what he's up to, if he's legit or a vulture. Do you want me to pass on your email?

Did you ever finish your documentary? All that footage. I'd much prefer your take on it all to this Dylan Charles. I know she would, too. Maybe we could Zoom sometime?

Love,
Katxx

Burn Your Flags

I can't reply. I have to reply. Any move means acknowledging it. Acknowledging Kat, my past, Manako. Letting her ghost back into my life. Manako never met Eri Kennedy or even Eri Kanehara. What would she say? With her sneer, her scorn, my life now. A foreign husband who never comes home, a bar owner who drinks too much, I run a language school and live in domesticity with tomatoes and potatoes in the garden. I own trees. What would Manako say? What would she say if I let her out of her box?

My past has been creeping up on me recently, not just the flashes of neon and Kat's email. Like some water wheel turning over, my head is being dunked back into the end of the eighties, the beginning of the nineties, those years when the world ended, the world changed, my world, their world, it all ticked over, like the new millennium came a decade early. The bubble burst, the crash came and we're still living with it, a world recession on top of decades of stagflation and the students aren't coming to the school in their droves anymore, all that disposable income and optimism for the future gone. Or was it pessimism? The future is bleak so you're going to need all the help you can get, all the skills you can pack into one little body, so your child can fight for scraps from the global market. Even now, retrenchment. We can't fight, we can't compete at this level so let's not, let's give up, circle the wagons, big fish in a small pond once more. Up close the water in a puddle looks like an ocean. If you reduce your perspective, you can pretend clarity.

The mood out there, that's what's back. It feels like it did then, at least for me, for us, for the runaways and misfits in the squats and clubs of Tokyo, skating under the highway flyovers, sniffing glue in multi-storey car parks, fighting in the alleys and sleeping in Denny's with only enough for an orange juice. That mood is back. Nothing matters so everything matters. Nothing can happen so anything can happen. Freeters, Neets, a life without security because there is no security anymore.

Or maybe it's just me. What does the future hold? At best, more of the same. We've got the house, the mortgage, the family, such as it is, such as it's staying, what's next? We had normal and now in a few months there's no such thing as normal. New normal. Masks and hand gel and being stuck at home forever. Being with him, forever. The trajectory, that's what he calls it, we're all on a trajectory from the cradle to the grave, the question is always what's next? What if nothing's next, nothing new, just more and more and more of the same? Endless. This is it.

This is it.

With my drink I climb the stairs, push open the office door with a foot, stand on the threshold looking in at the darkness. The cupboard doors are closed and as long as they remain that way I can pretend I'm here for some other reason, here to dust, to get a book, to check some detail in the documents we have accumulated to prove we are alive. The details of our existence filed page by page in a cabinet from Ikea. I turn on the light. The cupboard is fitted, the entire length of the back wall, with three sliding doors. Behind the first one is bedding. Behind the second, our summer clothes, packed up for the moment and probably lying under a fallen futon. The third I haven't opened since I placed everything behind it when we moved in. Even then, I didn't open the tape-sealed cardboard boxes, five of them, or the two record flight cases. They come everywhere with me. My souvenirs, the only things I kept from that life once it ended.

There was a time when the future seemed possible. When the past was something to run from, the future something to run towards. When you have no future along the conventional paths, every other future seems possible. Now it's all conventional. I'm a wife. I run a business. I took my piercings out, covered my tattoos, dyed my hair a neutral colour. Another new me. Another reinvention. I wear a mask every day. This virus is nothing new. More of the same.

Manako would punch me in the fucking face.

I don't want to be a mother.

I don't want to run a business.

I don't want to be a grown-up.

I don't want to watch what I say.

I don't want to behave.

I want to let rip.

Get drunk.

Get fucked up.

Get fucked.

I don't want to be me anymore.

Just for one night I want to be Eri Kanehara again.

Not Eri Kennedy. Just for a while.

I changed myself once, erased a complete identity, created a new one.

Eri Kanehara; I can be her again. Or the one before, the one Manako knew.

How the hell did Kat find me?

Where do you go when the future is empty?

Back. You go back.

I step forward, place the flat of my hand on the door, feel it pulsing, feel her pulsing, a flash of neon blue, the smell of stale smoke. She's still alive in there, in the tapes no one's ever seen. The tapes Kat is emailing about.

In 1989 the streets of Koenji were paved with vomit. Or at least the street outside the club was, some of it mine. I was fifteen and had been in Tokyo for about two months but still hadn't learned to keep the drink and the pills and the powder in my stomach. Everyone has to learn to drink somewhere, and I learned there. I was living with Takeshi and the rest of the band in a tiny apartment in Shin-Okubo, Koreatown, but we really lived in the live houses of the city, dirty, dingy, dark music venues, shithole dives with sticky carpets and graffitied walls. A gig every night. Takeshi played guitar in three bands, bass in a fourth and sometimes sang with a fifth.

That night, the night I met Manako, was a single release party, a split seven-inch, one song apiece from Takeshi's band NZF and Burn Your Flags. There were four bands on the bill, Burn Your Flags on third, NZF headlining. It was during the second band's set – I forget the name – that I redecorated the pavement. Burn Your Flags were outside, drinking cheap shōchū from the convenience store and passing a joint back and forth. I wiped my mouth on my sleeve and reached a hand for the bottle, washed my mouth out and spat.

Burn Your Flags, a four-piece, had only been together a few months but were already making waves. NZF's drummer, Shogo, played with them, the bass player, Sachi, I recognised from the scene, but the other two I didn't know. The guitarist, I'd soon find out, was a foreigner, a Chilean called Kat Higueros, black hair with blonde roots, streaks of red and blue through it, tattoos, a pierced tongue. The other was the singer, Manako. Small, her hair cut short and spiked, dyed electric blue, eyebrow and nose rings, dark around her eyes. In the light I couldn't tell if it was make-up or natural. This sneer, which I came to realise was a permanent expression, her default setting. Resting fuck you face, she called it. She took a drag on her joint. Kat took the whisky from me and swigged.

'Sit down.' She spoke Japanese with an accent, the syllables rolling and swelling in a way I liked instantly. I crouched down, my back against the wall and took the joint from

Manako. Her arm was red and there was liquid on the floor. I looked closer, squinting in the light from the street. Her left arm was slashed, blood running from it like a tap had been left on. She saw me looking, angled her arm so I could read.

燃える. Burn, like garbage.

She waited for my reaction. I refused to give her the satisfaction, it was just what she wanted, her type, she'd do anything to disturb, to get attention.

'You're the groupie?'

'Fuck you.'

'Yeah, you're Takeshi's groupie. I heard about you. What are you, fourteen?'

I looked to Shogo, the drummer, for support, but he shrugged, You're on your own.

'So what if I am? What's it fucking matter to you? And I'm fucking fifteen.'

'Ooooh! Do you play?'

'Play what?'

'Play. An instrument. You know, fucking music?' She jabbed a thumb at the live house.

'No.'

'What do you do, then?'

'What do you mean, do?'

'The purpose of your existence. What is it?'

'The purpose of my existence?' This bitch was getting on my tits. I pointed at the puddle of vomit. 'I puke.'

Kat laughed, handed me the bottle again. 'I like this one. We're on in a minute. Sachi, give her the camera.'

Manako took the bottle from me. Sachi pulled a video camera from her backpack and pushed it at me.

'If you've finished puking, you can film our set,' said Manako.

'Film this,' I said, giving her the finger. But I took the camera, and her joint.

I filmed their set that night, and every night, filmed other bands as well. Filmmaking took me over: I stole a camera from one of the big appliance shops, pocketed tapes that I used and reused until they wore out. Smuggled out books on filmmaking and sneaked into cinemas to watch foreign films, weird Korean things with subtitles, French classics from the fifties and sixties, black-and-white Japanese films about duty and honour. But it was Masashi Yamamoto's *Carnival in the Night* that hit me hardest. Not the most sophisticated of movies but it spoke to fifteen-year-old Eri. It's about a woman who casts aside her role as a single mother and transforms into a punk singer. The film seeps anger and violence. Molten with bile. We were all full of bile then, in our scene, anger and bile and violence, and I wanted to make a film just like that, but truer, more honest. About us. I wanted to make a film about the people around me, about Manako and her band, about the side of Tokyo, of Japan, nobody was looking at. The bubble had yet to burst and we made our way through that city like infected cells through an artery – they'd have erased us from their shiny, wealthy world if they ever noticed us for more than a second. We were shadows in the corner of their eyes. I wanted to drive my camera right through their eyeballs and smash their skulls.

Lofty ideas for a fifteen-year-old runaway with a bag full of drugs and stolen film equipment, surviving by running out on restaurant checks and giving salarymen hand-jobs. But then I'd run away to escape being told how to live my life. To get a life. To explore and endure and develop. To become, somehow, free. Lofty ideas were all I had to keep me going between meals.

Burn Your Flags

Outside the club that first night I gave her the finger but when they got on-stage and the opening chords of "Red Lipstick" ground their way from Manako's amp, I was hooked. She sang about the men who had fucked up her life, men she hated, men she wanted to kill, she sang about her father, the you in all her songs that she'd never talk about offstage. It connected. Ripped into me. I started filming, the lens focusing this fire I felt in me, this fire that had made me leave home for all the reasons Manako was singing about, this fire that had been burning out of control until that music and that moment and that camera all came together.

That was when it felt good, when the future didn't seem so bad. When the present was all that mattered, when the past was the thing to escape.

Burn Your Flags played two or three nights a week on any stage that would have them. They practised every other night in the basement of the print shop where Shogo worked. I recorded it all, keeping what was good, taping over them arguing about chord changes and aborted attempts. I'd have kept everything but I couldn't steal enough tapes.

I kept the camera running between songs, smoking, walking down the street afterwards, the adrenaline of a successful session spilling out onto the sidewalks of the capital, the energy of a gig roiling down the streets like a tsunami. I moved out of Takeshi's and into Manako and Kat's shithole apartment, filming everything.

My nail slices through the old tape on one of the boxes and I half expect there to be nothing inside but dust. But no, there they are. The video tapes, labelled, ready. This box is safe; these tapes are the practices and the gaps. These were the pieces I was going to use between songs, a montage, a collage of interviews, soundbites, words of wisdom. When my camera started to become obsolete I transferred everything onto VHS. Now they, too, are obsolete. A glance at my watch; eight pm. The recycle shop is open until ten.

Do I head downstairs, grab my keys and drive the ten minutes to Hard Off, or do I close the cupboard and keep my promise never to let Manako out? To keep her buried forever.

Christmas Eve. That's when ghosts come out.

The engine's on and I'm swinging out onto the road before I can stop myself. The impulse to see her is too strong. The flash of neon blue I've been seeing for weeks somewhere in the rear-view, clearer.

Already I'm tasting the flavour of the first video I'll play: We're in the tiny apartment, the three of us. We'd dropped acid while a typhoon battered the city, out on the balcony screaming at the storm as it screamed at us. The camera set up on its tripod in the corner so I could forget about filming. Manako yelling into the night about nature and humanity.

'We're animals,' her voice barely audible on the video over the crack of the wind. 'Animals, nothing more than slugs and sloths and wasps and elephants. The same. This storm hits us all the same. What's the difference between hiding in a hole in the ground and hiding in a fucked-up, run-down apartment? The world's ending the same for us all. It can't be stopped. The sky is falling on our heads.'

She climbed onto the edge of the balcony, holding onto the roof for balance, her black skirt flapping like a bird, black leggings underneath drenched and heavy, boots squeaking. We wore shoes inside because it was rebellious but mainly because there was broken glass everywhere.

'It's the end of the world and what are we doing? China's shooting students, Europe is falling apart, the Soviet Union is falling apart. It's the end of the world. It can't be stopped.

Burn Your Flags

Hasn't gone far enough. The end point is obvious: no more nations. No more nationalities. No more borders. No more flags. Nations haven't been around forever. They're just where we are in the chain. Caves to villages to towns to cities to feudal alliances to nations. Who says it has to stop there? An end to nations means an end to nationalism. An end to racism. Intermixing, intermarrying, interbreeding. All the world as one race called humanity. No passports, no visas, no borders. Go where you want. Live where you want. Do what you want. What does it leave?'

She leaped back off the balcony, splashing Kat and me.

'And what does that leave? Animals. Burn your flags. Burn your passports and your birth certificates. Be who you want to be.'

She stabbed at the camera, passion in her eyes, anger lining her face.

'Burn your fucking flags!'

I download the software, connect my brand new antique video recorder to the capture device I got at Hideki Denki and connect that to my computer, start transferring everything for the second time. But something about it doesn't feel right. Digital's too clean for this. This isn't cinema in the Netflix age, this is archaeology. I stop the transfer and press play on the VHS.

Maybe digital is the last storage form we use; maybe in a couple of decades I'll be transferring them again to a chip in my skull or an implant in my eyeball. The technology people are talking about already, touch screens like cling film that you can wrap along your arm, turn your skin into a screen. Head-up displays in glasses. Turning us into cyborgs. It's inevitable. I mean, say you're in a car crash, you lose your legs, crushed, you lose a hand, cut clean off by some shard of metal. Your airbag fails and a blow to the head damages your eyesight. Your doctor offers you robotic feet and a hand, would you take them? Of course, why even ask? And retinal implants. We can make you see again, Mrs Kennedy, with these robotic eyes. Tempted? Fuck yes, get these passed-it squishy things out of my head and let me get a good look at you. Technologising the body, one car crash at a time. Then what? Aural implants to translate any language? My business goes under, no language teachers required. It's going that way, people using their phones and Google translate like an inanimate interpreter. And after that? Brain implants. Neural lace. Wi-Fi-enabled brains so you can access any information just by thinking about it? I'm not sure I'd like that, the idea of brain surgery, of foreign bodies in there, but you always get early adopters. Rich parents want to give their kids an advantage. Why spend every evening in a cram school when a few million yen and an operation later your offspring can waltz through the Tokyo University entrance exam without ever opening a book? So the rich kids get implanted and straightaway you have a segregated classroom, a way of dividing students that is only going to lead to more bullying. Next the middle class parents, whether to keep up with the richer kids, or to save their own from being bullied, they remortgage their house, save up the bonuses, and get their children implanted as well. Pretty soon only the poor kids are without and testing in school is abandoned because what's the point? All you're testing is the network's bandwidth. Prices come down and eventually even the poor kids can get implanted and now you have a full generation with implanted brains. Chipped. Then you just wait for the grandparents and parents to die, and the human race is chipped, implanted, half-robot. And this isn't science fiction. This is technology being developed now. Available now. This is something for the next generation. Our children. If we had children, this would be an issue for Cormac and me. But that's not going to happen. Let Saki and Honoka worry about it. I'm done with babies and technology. If it is the end of the world – and Manako was adamant about it back then, what would she have made of the pandemic? – then why bring any more life into it just to suffer?

No future.

The labels don't make sense until I start watching one labelled "Giraffes?". What the fuck is giraffes? Then in the video, there's a giraffe. Two of them. Outside a car dealership, for some unknown reason, they are using fibreglass giraffes to sell cars. One is taller than the other, a parent, maybe, or a partner, a stereotype marriage with a big, strong boy giraffe out ahead and a small, meek girl giraffe trailing a few steps behind. Manako up on the front one, standing on its back, a circus performer, a diminutive general leading her troops into battle. Kat sits behind her, whipping it to a gallop with a switch she ripped off a tree on our way through the park. Shogo has his trousers round his ankles and is hanging off the back of the second giraffe like a sex-mad koala while Sachi spray-paints FREE ALL GIRAFES across its side. The footage cuts out as the sound of sirens filters in from the night.

Next is an interview with Kat. She's holding her yellow Gibson Les Paul Jr with the Chilean flag under the strings. We were sitting in the apartment. Behind her the shredded plasterboard, light fittings hanging loose, the kitchen window that didn't close on one side, the other smashed, filled in with cardboard and bin liners. Manako and Sachi had covered the walls in art and slogans. Walls as canvas. A tin of white paint handy for when they got bored with one piece and wanted to start again. Sachi had started art school but smoked more and more marijuana until she flunked out. She was good, though, could free-draw birds perfectly, and covered the roof, Sistine Chapel-like, in birds on branches. Manako went more for provocative slogans and occasional graphic sexual imagery. Camera on the tripod, I ask Kat questions from the armchair, legs tucked under myself, trying to roll a joint. I was shit at it but wanted to learn. One of those skills I figured it would be good to have.

'So why did you come to Japan?'

'Because I could. My great-grandfather emigrated from Japan to Chile at the beginning of this century to work in the mines. He took his wife with him and started a family. My mother is descended from that line but my father is Chilean. That's why I've got two names, Higueros and Hayashida.'

'So you're a half?'

'Don't call me that. It's fucking stupid. I'm not less than whole. I'm not less than anything.'

'But that's the Japanese word.'

'So? Language reinforces discrimination. Men and women use different registers here so discrimination against women perpetuates. Calling someone a half makes them seem less than they are, so you are justified in treating them differently. If anything I'm more. I'm a double. There are two of me. Japanese Kat and Chilean Kat.'

'I'm going to call you Ziggy,' Sachi says off-camera. 'You're some Kat from Japan.' She comes into shot, finds a space on the wall and begins sketching out a giant welcome cat, one of those waving things they have in shop windows. I turn the camera on her, a spliff in her mouth as she draws and then paints. She gives the cat Bowie's Aladdin Sane face paint and Kat's yellow Gibson.

It's three in the morning when I hear Cormac's car pull in.

I've watched three of the videos, all early stuff, rehearsals, scenes in the apartment, atmospheric shots walking down dark alleys and overlooking busy highways. The plum wine is gone. I open some of the sake we got in Kochi and were saving.

One of the boxes is filled with albums, seven-inch singles and cassettes. Fortunately vinyl is one thing Cormac and I still agree on, so the stereo separates are all top quality, set up and ready to go. I haul them into the office trailing cables behind me. Cormac's car crunches into the drive just as I'm flipping "Stop Jap" by The Stalins. I haven't listened to any of this stuff in years. Too much nostalgia. I mostly listen to jazz or classical these days. Anything I can ignore. The only vinyl on the living room shelves is Cormac's, of course.

I place the needle on side B. This is going to lead to a conversation at some point. Everything fucking does with him. We have to talk about fucking everything. He can't just be quiet. Can't let things go. He's more of a woman than I am. More of a stereotype, anyway.

'You're up late. Having a party?'

'I thought I'd have the place to myself.' I can hear a slur in there.

'Sorry to ruin your fun. You know you can hear this halfway down the street. I'm surprised no one's called the cops.'

'Sounds like a job for you.' I slap the volume up.

'What's got into you?'

'Nothing for weeks.'

He empties his pockets. Coins into one bowl. Keys into another. Sorts out his receipts, one pile for business expenses, one for our shared expenses, another for the bin. Throws today's mask into the garbage.

'Why didn't you come home?'

'I didn't want to fight.'

'You're the one who that's always going on about communication. How we need to talk. How can we talk if you're not here?'

'We never talk even when I am here.'

'Yes, yes, it's all my fault, I'm a bad wife, I don't think about others, I don't know how you put up with me.'

'Don't say that, you know that's not what I mean. I just mean that it's communication. Everything is communication. We have to communicate. Almost all problems can be solved by talking about them.'

'Not all.'

'Almost all. Yes, all. I can't think of an example that couldn't at least be made better by discussing it. It's such a frustrating Japanese trait. You all do it, I've seen it so many times in meetings. An issue is raised and everyone sits in silence contemplating it and no one speaks until they've made up their own mind. Everyone is scared to speak unless they're sure they have the correct answer. It starts in school, you're taught to listen, memorise and answer the question correctly. No discussion. No debate. No proffering ideas. New ideas come from the synthesis of a number of different ideas. If you never have the discussion, you never come up with anything new. This is why the economy has been stagnating for nearly three decades. Because no one talks about anything. They just keep their thoughts to themselves and bide their time until they can make the decisions. And you do it, too. Like when we want to go on holiday. I offer five or six ideas and you say nothing, don't discuss the pros and cons, just sit like you're not even listening and then a few days later say, "Right, I've decided. I want to go to Taiwan."'

'You're turning into one of those foreigners.'

'What?'

'You told me to tell you when you were turning into one of

those foreigners you hate, the ones who make generalisations about the Japanese and complain about the society here. You said, "I hate those fuckers. If I ever start talking like that, kill me.""

'I-'

'So can I kill you now?'

'If you like.'

Exasperated, that look where he thinks he's not getting through to me, that I don't understand him. I do understand, I just disagree. I turn away, pour another drink.

'What have you been doing, anyway? What's this video recorder for?'

'I'm going to make a documentary.' I didn't even mean to say that. I'm not going to make anything. But something about the idea, the sentence…

'You? What are you talking about?'

'I used to be a filmmaker. You didn't know that about me, did you? Hidden depths. Not just a wife and a manager –'

'I never said –'

'Yeah, anyway, I've decided I'm going to finish a film I started years ago.'

'From your Tokyo days? Is that what this one-woman mosh pit is in aid of?' He picks up the NZF/Burn Your Flags split seven-inch. I nearly grab it from him, electricity between his touch and the disc. Two parallel universes crashing together, something that defies the laws of physics, that should never happen. Instead I step back.

'Put it on.' He plays it. Music was our common ground, from the day we met in Club Rock N Roll. A safe space.

'This is good. Who is it?' He turns the cover over. 'I've never heard of them.'

'It's Manako,' I said. 'She's dead.'

Cormac goes to bed and I switch off the music and return to

the videos. Did I mean what I said? Am I really going to edit this all together? Make that film I promised her? It would at least be better than this Dylan Charles doing it. Google reveals him to be as bad as I feared: edgy, controversial, revisionist. A documentary maker who thinks the star of the show is him. He'll have spent years hunting for a story that no one knows. A scandal. A mystery. Radical youth culture and a death in Tokyo. A Netflix wet dream. I can see him now, sitting at his editing suite, top-of-the-range equipment and his awards prominently displayed with over-emphasised subtlety, with a big fucking hard-on about the cute little Japanese punk girl he can discover and save from obscurity.

Well, not without me he isn't. No one knows what happened. Not really. Not completely. Not even the rest of the band. No one knows how she died. No one. Not even me. Manako was alone in that basement, just her and my camera.

NZF recorded an album and organised a tour of Japan, taking Burn Your Flags along as openers. Two bands, two vans, from Tokyo up to Hokkaido, then back along the Sea of Japan and down to Kansai, along the Shinkansen line to Fukuoka, down to Kyushu and back again. It took the best part of a month, sleeping in vans between equipment and feet, crashing in random hovels offered by fans. Takeshi and I were done so I stayed with the girls, recording everything as we went. One tape has a show in Osaka in this basement room. Looks like a sex dungeon but someone's stuck a stage at one end and a fridge of beer at the other. We had no money – nothing to sell and no ticket money to speak of, or at least none Burn Your Flags ever saw – and being cooped up together all day and all night led to violent outbursts. Men at the gigs would leer and grab the band. Kat broke one guy's nose with her guitar, spraying blood across its yellow body. She didn't clean it off; a warning to others. In Kumamoto some dick pushed his way on-stage and started dancing with Manako. She headbutted him, then beat him with the microphone stand, stomped up and down on him while the rest of the band tried to play on. His friends jumped onstage. The band stopped and joined in the melee. NZF piled in and the whole thing turned into a riot. We ran when the cops showed up. The next morning Takeshi and Shogo broke into the venue and got the gear back, as well as a couple of crates of beer. The beer they are drinking in the video of the last show in Kagoshima.

I wake up slumped on the desk and it takes me a moment to work out where I am and why. Cormac's car backs out and speeds off. He'll be in a bad mood. He likes to pretend Christmas doesn't mean anything to him anymore, that it's just for kids, but he'll be upset I wasn't awake to say Merry Christmas. Recently he's been worse than usual, more childish, needing constant attention and reassurance. Fuck him.

My head is splitting. Plum wine and sake is a bad mix. As I get older hangovers are getting more existential. Before there'd be a headache and some nausea, now the main symptom is paranoia. What did I do? Who did I offend? What have I lost?

I make some coffee and go back to the office. The heating has been on all night, it's the only room in the house that isn't freezing. Still, I pull a blanket off the bed and wrap myself in it. I can't watch any more for now so I set up the transfer. It runs in real time, will take days to upload everything. If I digitise everything. There's one tape, one tape at the bottom of the last box, the tape that was in the camera in the studio. The only one I've never watched.

By the start of 1990, Burn Your Flags had made a name for themselves on the scene. They had a new drummer, Yayoi. They weren't famous – they never would be, not in Japan – but for those who cared, they were important. Fanzines interviewed them. People started to know the words and sing along at the gigs. They bootlegged themselves, recorded shows on shitty tape machines and sold them the next week. We stole blank t-shirts and scrawled slogans on them, sold them as merch. Anything to scrape together a bit of cash to pay for studio time. These days they'd crowdfund, or use credit cards, but back then there was none of that and studios were expensive, even the ones friendly to the scene. But we did it – I say we because I was so much part of the band by now – and managed to get the cheapest hours available, usually around six am when no one wants to make music. They recorded four tracks and released the *Burn it Down EP*. My copy was kissed by every band member while they wore the brightest, most ridiculous lipstick, four bright kisses.

That was the high point, that EP. They had enough material for a double album at least but that would never happen. A split seven-inch and an EP the sole legacy of Burn Your Flags, of Manako's output, of her revolution. There were only a few hundred of each and vinyl is easily broken. None of it is on YouTube. Art is ephemeral. The whole point is the moment, the experience, being in the room, being at that gig. Even as I recorded everything I knew I was capturing shadows. It isn't the footage that matters, it's the memories the footage sparks. Kat's laugh. Sachi's encyclopaedic knowledge of rock music. Yayoi's friendly openness, a bright sun in an otherwise dark world. And Manako's fire, an energy burning so hot it couldn't last forever. It's how I know Dylan Charles is a vampire – this isn't nostalgia for him, or for anyone. For those who weren't there, there's nothing to be nostalgic about.

Burn Your Flags

Just a mystery. A romantic, filthy, beautiful, heroic rock and roll death.

Sales of the EP and our usual scams meant we would be able to record again by the summer of 1990. The band's idea was to have everything written, everything prepped, everything note perfect before setting foot in the studio. That way they could play everything a couple of times and get an album done in two or three days. Play it live, capture the energy of the band. No overdubs. No double-tracking, just raw punk rock. In and out.

They had plenty of songs but Manako wasn't happy. They'd been playing them every day for a year, whether live or at practice, and she was bored. It was supposed to be about the moment, the song you're playing now, and the next one, not the last one. That was already played. That had already been heard. Pushed herself to write more and more, to dig deeper into her creativity. She wasn't sleeping but then none of us did apart from Yayoi, who could sleep through an earthquake. She was taking drugs, so many drugs we had no idea whether she was coming up or down. Manic. Crashing. But we didn't notice because so were we.

They were still using the basement of the print shop to practise. Shogo's father owned it and seemed quite relaxed at all the freaks coming in and out. The only rule was that we stayed out of the way during opening hours. In the run-up to recording the album Manako got round this by not leaving. Even when NZF were practising she sat in the corner writing lyrics. I brought her food, drink, cigarettes and filmed her improvisations, her rants, her quiet monologues.

The last thing I recorded and watched was one of these monologues. Manako was subdued, downbeat that day. It was two, maybe three nights before her death. Slouched on a battered armchair covered with blankets, her Telecaster draped over her, she'd strum it gently as she spoke, as if accompanying herself, singing the blues.

'I was a little rich girl,' she says. 'My father is a politician, something in the government. I try not to know. He... well, you know what he did. You've heard my songs. But he was respectable. A public figure. A reputation. I went to an expensive private school, all privilege and bullying. Made it to the second grade of junior high school.'

Me too, I nodded. 'You dropped out?'

'Kicked out. I mean, deservedly, but still. The school was elite, girls only, the training ground for the wives of the powerful since Meiji something. There was no sense of future ambition or potential, just simple rigid structures based on age and primacy. Basic Confucianism, good old-fashioned patriarchy.

'Usual gangs and cliques. The main gang was led by this girl Sakura. Her father was also a politician, much higher, much more powerful than mine. There were two sisters, Sakura and Yumemi. Sakura was the bully; Yumemi the weak one. Older and younger. So it goes. Yumemi was in my class. Sakura was two years older. A senior while we were first grade. She ran the school, her and her officially sanctioned army. About twenty of them, all kendo students, marched around the school with their wooden swords, policing. The slightest infringement of rules got you a crack on the head, a jab in the ribs. And like all armies, like all police forces, they were corrupt, on the make. Money was extorted, snacks, electronic devices, anything that took their fancy. The authorities smiled on it all. Students cowed by fear are easier to handle. With kids controlling each other, there was less need for teacher involvement, more time for relaxing, more time to concentrate on indoctrination of their ideology. Sakura was a ringleader, circus master, and we graduated from elementary school into her world.

'Being friends with Yumemi didn't protect you. It made you a target. Sakura loathed everyone but she hated her sister most of all. We thought she'd be safe but actually she was targeted more than the rest of us. Everything from being tripped in the corridor to a head down the toilet to her clothes being stolen during sports. There were no neutrals at that school, but Yumemi was the biggest victim.

'It was only a matter of time before they went too far. The first day back after the summer vacation Hiroko Imaeda, the daughter of a diplomat, a nerdy kid who had grown up overseas and struggled with kanji, made the mistake of not immediately surrendering her comic to one of Sakura's goons. With a split skull, broken fingers and a cracked rib she left in an ambulance and never came back. For a couple of weeks everything paused, the whole school was suspended in the moment before a rollercoaster drops, waiting for something, for Hiroko's father to do something, for the police, for other parents, for anything to happen. A reporter turned up and left with an envelope stuffed with cash, at least that was the rumour. That was it. If the principal ever spoke to Sakura about it, Yumemi never learned.

'The school authorities, in their inaction, gave Sakura permission to do what she liked. There was no line she couldn't cross. She was above the law. Yumemi disagreed. She'd liked Hiroko. They liked the same manga and anime. Swapped books. Regardless of what the principal thought, we all knew something had to be done. Sakura would graduate to high school the following April but at that age six months is a lifetime. Yumemi decided to take a stand. We couldn't fight back with violence – we'd lose. But there was one thing the school valued above all else: its reputation.

'It was remarkably easy to take over the library.' She laughs, grinds out the cigarette. 'It occupied the whole top floor of the main tower and was ideal – we were alone and able to see in every direction; there were only two doorways and no one above. We got both the librarians into the elevator, hands tied behind their backs. Yumemi explained what we were doing to those who were in the library studying, and only a handful opted to leave with the staff. We barricaded the doors with bookshelves, jammed the elevator doors open, and smashed the vending machines to provide sustenance for the long struggle ahead. We pulled posters off the wall and emptied the stationary cupboard looking for anything to make banners with. DOWN WITH FASCISM, NO MORE VIOLENCE and JUSTICE FOR IMAEDA. Yumemi made a series of signs personally insulting Sakura, calling into question her chastity, accusing her of bed-wetting, of being a whore. Over the days that followed Yumemi wrote a series of leaflets outlining the more embarrassing moments of Sakura's childhood and dropped the defamatory confetti on the students and staff below. After years of abuse she had turned the tap on, and there was no way of turning it off.

'It was my awakening, too. I started reading anything I could find in the library on struggle, on rebellion. We needed educating, and fast. We needed a manifesto, a framework, an ideology. I learned about the almost-revolution of the sixties, about how our parents took to the streets and then when it was all over, took jobs in the system they swore to smash.

'The first day and night were fun. It was probably the only time the library had heard that much laughter. As we outlined strategy for the struggle, making lists of demands, fleshing out arguments, we were all in high spirits. We held the library for five days. After the first night, the tension dissipated. A few of the girls made a domino rally out of books, quite a spectacular one, up and down furniture, in and out of cupboards, through shelves. We found a deck of cards. Someone started a competition to see who could find the funniest line in a book. You opened it at random and read the first sentence you saw. That lasted about ten minutes. No one won.

'I kept reading. Trotsky, Marx, Che, Maruyama, Oda, Yoshimoto. Started writing down quotes and dropping them out the window. Made speeches no one could possibly hear. I soon grew tired; retreated to the history section and set about defacing and rewriting all the books I disagreed with.

'As boredom increased, morale fell. The vending machines held little choice. Some began to regret remaining and discussed leaving. The rest of us talked them out of it. In the end no one left, but the idea infected everyone, and reduced morale further.

'Most of our entertainment came from watching the crowd outside. We'd brought the school to a standstill and with nothing better to do, our schoolmates stood looking up at us. There were brief bursts of excitement, like when Sakura and her gang attacked the barricades. They battered the doors with baseball bats and metal rods, heaved their weight against it. Looked like they might break through, but the stairwell was narrow and the shelves heavy; they just couldn't get enough weight into the push, and it would've taken a month to break the fire containment doors down. In the end they resigned themselves to detailed descriptions of what they would do when we finally came out. We had to come out sometime. The staff had no intention of negotiating; we later found out the principal had gone golfing.

'Eventually they had to put their public image to one side in the hope of a solution. The police were called in, and with them the reporters. The sight of police cars pulling into the playground raised anxiety levels a few notches, but it also made us kind of proud: we were being taken seriously. It was the closest we came to victory. The story of Imaeda and the bullying couldn't be kept secret anymore. Our parents had initially kept their distance from the whole thing – so many of them with reputations to think about – but once the details of how the school was being run and exactly what had happened to Imaeda emerged, sympathy shifted. Even those who approved of rigid discipline, enforced physically if necessary, felt things had gone a little far. The golf didn't help.

'Of course we didn't know this at the time. We just knew we were getting hungry and tired, bored and frustrated and worried. We were all going to be in serious trouble when this was over. With our parents, with the school, with the police. There was no way it could end well.

'The end finally came after a night without power or water: when we realised the toilets wouldn't flush, we pretty much gave up. The smell was revolting. We didn't announce our exit, just quietly got into the elevators and appeared suddenly before the cameras. We could see Sakura itching to get at us, but they'd been warned by the principal not to do anything while the police and the cameras were there. As we passed, Sakura waved at her sister.

'We were all immediately arrested, though Yumemi managed to make a statement to the cameras about smashing fascism, pleaded for justice for Imaeda. The rest of us meekly got into the police cars, keeping our heads down, avoiding the limelight.

'Home was unbearable. Father beat me for compromising his position, the family's reputation, wheeling out the clichés and the self-righteous smugness. But I got off lightly. Yumemi hung herself the night she got home.

'That's when I left. I knew I'd do the same. It was only a matter of time before someone said something, before I was triggered, before he'd touch me… It was only a matter of time.'

She gets up and walks out of shot. I remember sitting there, unable to move. I wanted to hug her. To tell her my story. I wanted to show her my scars, show her she wasn't alone. But she was alone. We both were. We're all alone, forever. Nothing I could say or do would ever change that. I knew that then. She knew it. You could only resist for so long. Every nail that sticks out gets hammered down eventually. It's only a matter of time.

I left the camera there in the basement, it being safer than where we were living. It was on, running, recording, when I found her, it's red light unblinking in the face of all that blood.

I tidied up before calling anyone. Took away the camera, her lyrics, the pick she'd been using. Stashed it all in a coin locker at Shinagawa Station before returning and finding her all over again. I picked it all up when I jumped on a local JR train heading west. By the time I got to Nagoya I was Eri Kanehara.

While the videos transfer I tidy up the mess from last night, myself included. Cormac must be hiking; his boots are gone from their spot by the door. A cobweb lies limply where they used to stand. We should do an end-of-year clean but that's something for another day. I should be thinking about New Year's resolutions. I can't ever remember what I thought last year. Get in shape. Eat healthy. Some shit like that. Why do we make resolutions? It's just a calendar changing, nothing else. The only thing separating January 1 from December 31 is convention. No start and no end, just an endless unrolling of days. I shower and put the washing on, hang it up outside where it's crisp but dry. He texts about dinner. I can't think about it, don't want to think about it, don't want to make any decisions.

I'm not cooking.

I'll cook. Was thinking about a stew. Warm winter food.

I might have to go out.

Let me know.

I don't reply. I don't reply to him. I haven't replied to Kat. Why is she meeting this Dylan Charles? Why bring it all up? Why include me?

If I speak to him, the walls crumble. If I do anything with the videos, the walls crumble.

They're already coming down. Kat found me. She connected Eri Kennedy with Eri Kanehara, with that girl she knew in Tokyo all those years ago. I need to decide. I can't decide. What do I want?

Twenty-five years. A lot of water under a lot of bridges.

I don't want to be a mother.

I don't want to run a business.

I don't want to be a grown-up.

I don't want to watch what I say.

I don't want to behave.

I don't want to be me anymore.

I want to let rip.

Where do you go when the future is empty?

Back. You go back.

Acknowledgments

Without the enthusiasm, support and encouragement of Paul and Angela Docherty, this story would still be languishing on a hard drive. Thanks to Christian Livermore, for excellent editorial advice and catching all my errors. Thanks to Ian F. Martin for answering my questions on the Tokyo punk scene. Thanks to Kirstin Innes and J. David Simons for their kind words and support. Thanks to my agent, Judy Moir, for comments on the early draft and clear-headed advice throughout. Finally thanks to Minori, for being nothing like Eri even when I am occasionally like Cormac. Their marriage is nothing like ours, for which I am grateful.

This story was drafted over a weekend at the end of 2020.

Other Books by Liminal Ink

My Heart's Content

On Christmas Day 2013, **Angela Hughes** received an unusual gift: a new heart. Her memoir is a fearless account of her wait, in hospital, for a donor. Contrary to expectations, moments of joy and laughter are plentiful. When all tomorrows are fading fast, real strength comes from a renewed appreciation of the things that truly matter.

About Liminal Ink

Formed by Angela and Paul Docherty, Liminal Ink is a tiny, independent publisher on the Scottish coast, where the River Tay meets the North Sea, where shallow meets deep, where fresh meets salt. The blurred line where one thing ends and another begins.

What if? Paul asked. Why not? Angela replied. And the seed of an idea germinated and grew.

Liminal Ink is a leap of faith; a creative project born out of curiosity and a longing to soften those boundaries between writer and publisher. It's about collaboration and exploration. A belief that by working together we can create something more than the sum of its parts.

liminalink.com
Words @ work & play